I HAVE ALWAYS BEEN FASCINATED BY EVERYTHING ELIZABETHAN:
THE CLOTHES, THE MUSIC, THE DANCING, THE FOOD. WHEN I HAD THE
IDEA FOR A STORY ABOUT A YOUNG BOY WHO IS FLUNG THROUGH TIME
TO LAND ON THE STAGE OF THE GLOBE THEATRE IN TUDOR LONDON,
I SAW MY CHANCE TO SHARE THOSE HARSH, DIRTY, BRUTAL, BEAUTIFUL
TIMES WITH OTHERS. I MADE MY WAY THROUGH A MOUNTAIN OF BOOKS
TO DISCOVER ALL THE AMAZING HISTORICAL DETAILS OF THE ERA; THEN
I DRAFTED AND REDRAFTED THE STORY TO MAKE IT RICH AND REAL.

ONE OF THE THINGS I LEARNED WAS THAT SHAKESPEARE'S PLAYS WERE
PERFORMED AT FOUR O'CLOCK ON MIDSUMMER AFTERNOONS. THAT WAS
WHEN I KNEW I HAD THE KEY TO THE MAGIC IN THIS BOOK.

GREGORY ROGERS

# The BOY, The BEAR, The BARON, The BARD

## GREGORY ROGERS

A NEAL PORTER BOOK
ROARING BROOK PRESS
BROOKFIELD, CONNECTICUT

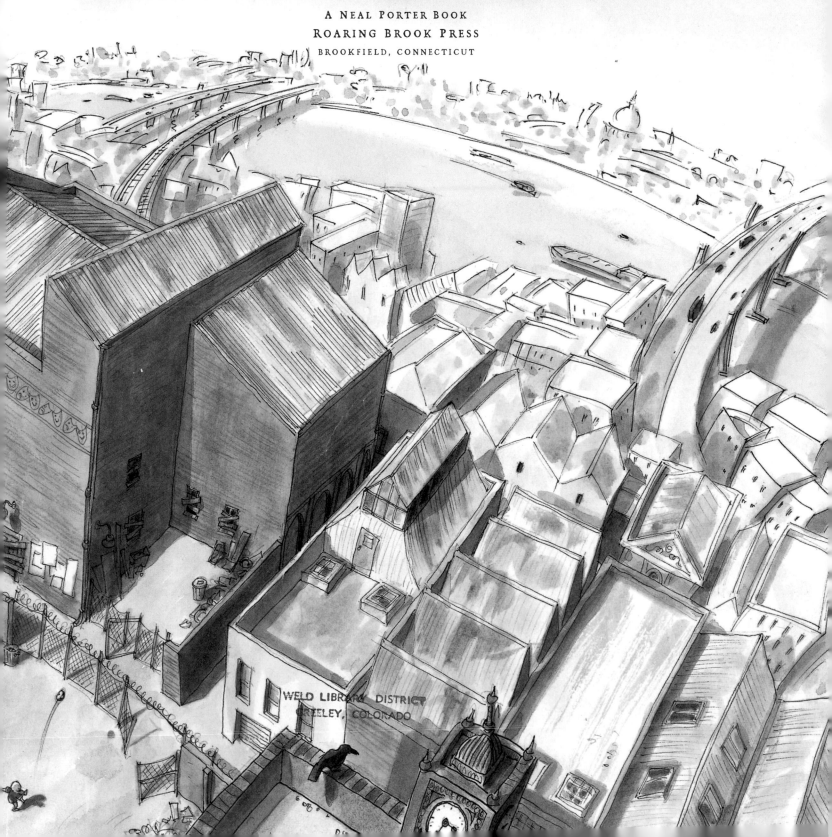

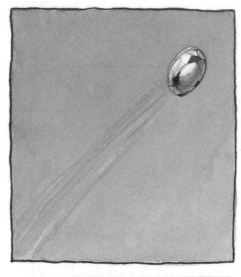

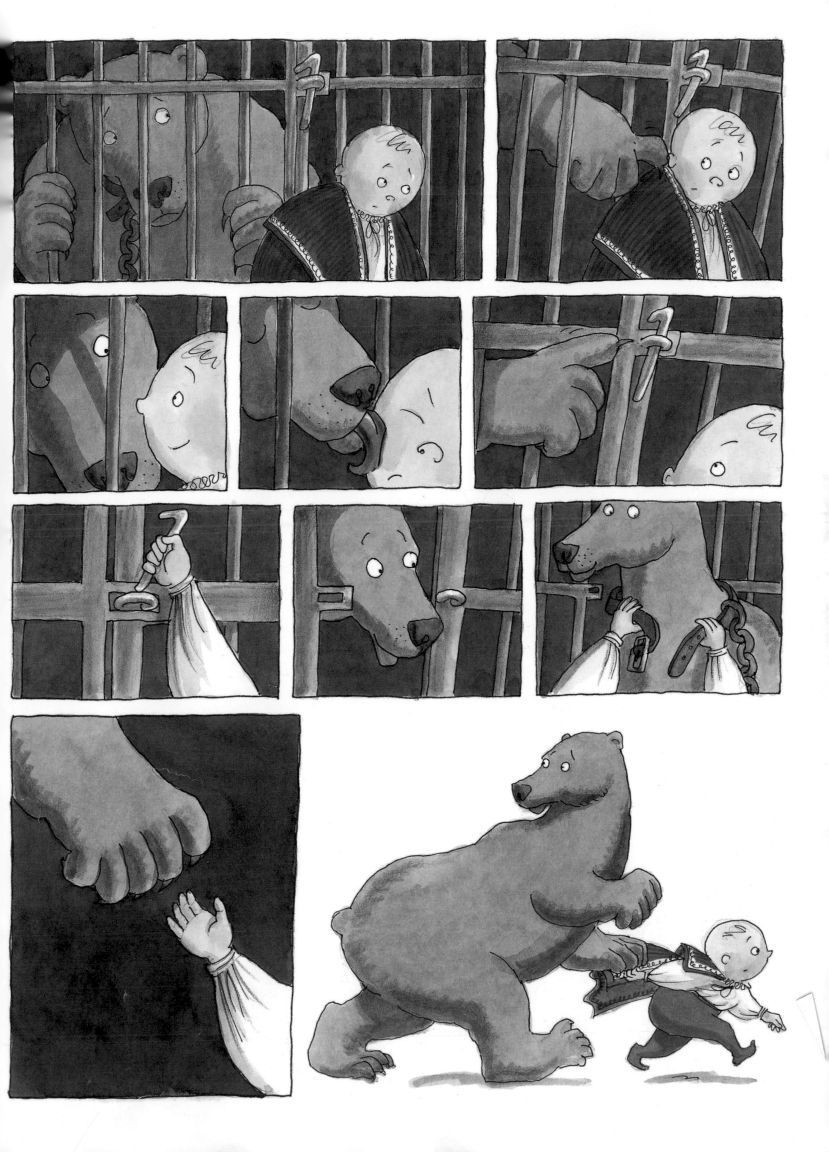

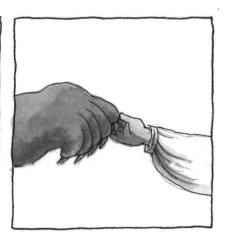

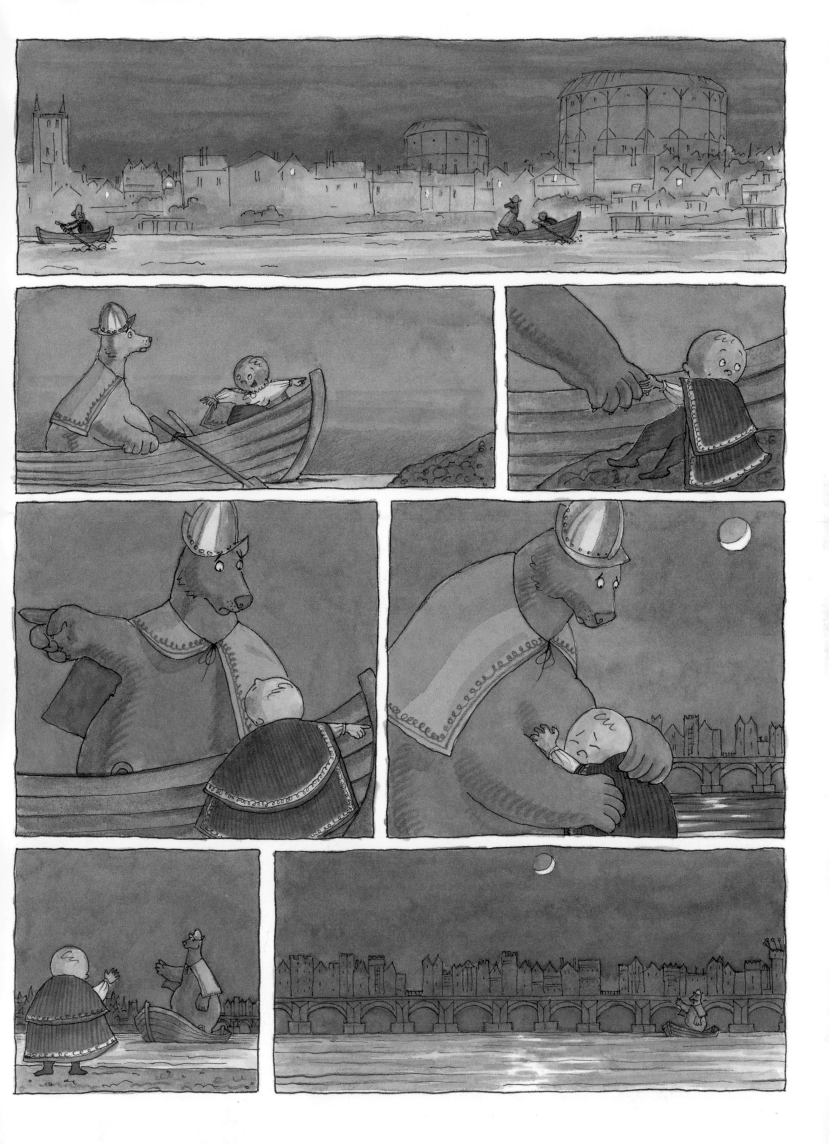

## ACKNOWLEDGEMENTS

I want to thank all those people who helped me to make
this book a reality. Thanks Jenny Thynne for your help with
all things British, Margaret Connolly for being the best agent
in the world and Jodie Webster for your keen eye that can spot
a fumble at fifty paces. Thanks Neal Porter for showing faith
in the new kid on the block. And thanks to my supporters on
the home front, Bart, Harry and Pudding.